Night Night, Woolly

Lift me up . . . .

For Carrie and Penny

WOOLLY AND TIG: NIGHT NIGHT, WOOLLY
A BANTAM BOOK 978 0 857 51335 9

Published in Great Britain by Bantam,
an imprint of Random House Children's Publishers UK
A Random House Group Company.

This edition published 2013

1 3 5 7 9 10 8 6 4 2

WOOLLY AND TIG created by Brian Jameson.
WOOLLY AND TIG word and device marks are trade marks of Tattiemoon Limited and are used under license.
WOOLLY AND TIG device marks © Tattiemoon Limited 2011.
The "BBC" word mark and logo are trade marks of the British Broadcasting Corporation and are used under license.
BBC logo © BBC 2012, licensed by Tattiemoon Limited.
Woolly and Tig is produced for CBeebies by Tattiemoon in association with CharacterShop.
With special thanks to Dr Martin Williams.

Bantam Books are published by Random House Children's Publishers UK,
61–63 Uxbridge Road, London W5 5SA

www.**randomhousechildrens**.co.uk

Addresses for companies within The Random House Group Limited can be found at:
www.randomhouse.co.uk/offices.htm

THE RANDOM HOUSE GROUP Limited Reg. No. 954009

A CIP catalogue record for this book is available from the British Library

Printed in China

Night Night, Woolly

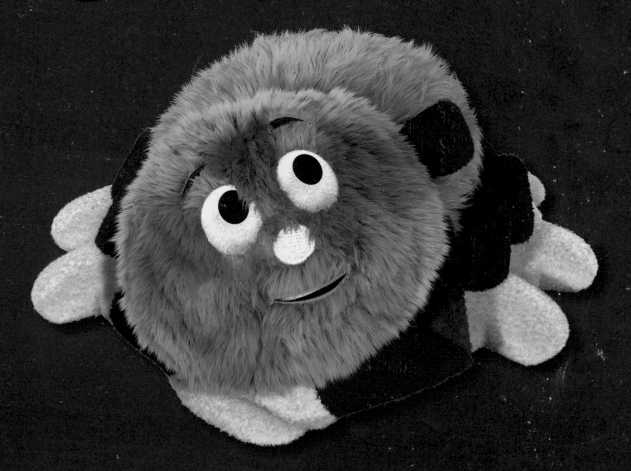

Brian Jameson

Bantam

Hey, I'm Woolly!
I'm fluffy, and I'm happy, and I'm a toy spider.

You can see I'm fluffy, but how do you know I'm happy?

Yes, because I'm smiling!

You made me smile!

This is Tig in her bed.
I'm Tig's favourite toy so I'm in her bed too.
Hooray!
But why is Tig not smiling?
"I don't like the dark," says Tig.

Tig's Daddy bought Tig a lamp to put by her bed.
Tig took the lamp out of a box.
"My very own light," said Tig.
"No worries in the dark now," said Daddy.

Tig and Daddy took the lamp into Tig's bedroom. Tig switched the lamp on.

"I like my new lamp," said Tig.
But the lamp wasn't much fun in the day.
"I want it to be dark," said Tig.

Lift me up . . .

Tig was excited. While she waited for bedtime, Tig made a puppet theatre with the box the lamp came in.

"I like doing puppet shows," said Tig.

When it was dark and bedtime came, Tig switched on her new lamp.
"Time for my puppet show," said Tig.

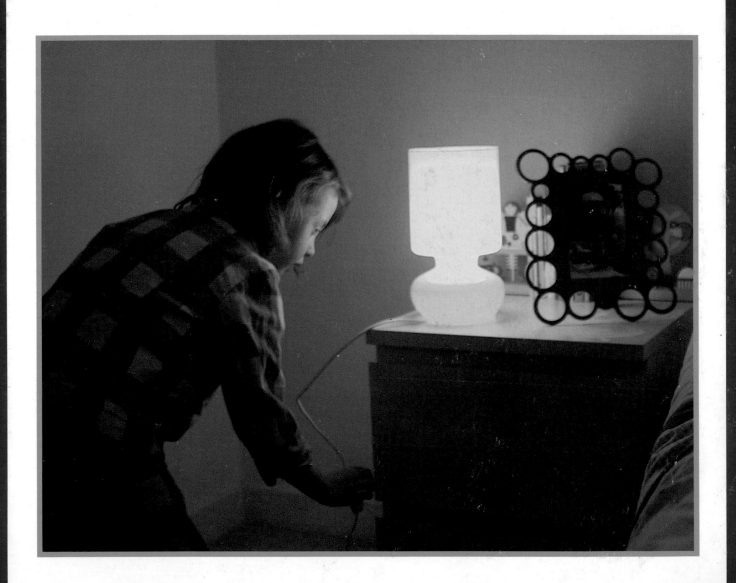

Lift me up ...

Mummy and Daddy came to watch Tig's puppet show.
"Two puppet birds fly away!" shouted Tig.

"Well done, Tig," said Mummy and Daddy.
"What a great puppet show!"
Tig liked doing puppet shows. Tig was happy.
I liked Tig's puppet show too.

You made me smile!

"Time to snuggle down," said Mummy.
"Can I have my new lamp on all night?"
said Tig.

"Of course you can, Tig,"
said Mummy. "We'll leave
the big light on too."

Lift me up

When Tig was fast asleep, Daddy tiptoed into the bedroom and switched the big light off.

"Night-night, Tig," he whispered. "Sleep tight."

Tig's new lamp glowed in the dark beside her bed.

Tig's little bedroom was all cosy and snug in the night, and I snuggled down all cosy next to her.

Lift me up . . .

That night Tig woke up. It was dark, but Tig's new lamp glowed light.

"I like my new lamp," said Tig. "I don't mind the dark."
Tig felt safe.

But when Tig looked up
at the ceiling there was
something else new.
There were monsters,
hairy monsters, running
round and round!
Tig wasn't happy. Tig felt
frightened!

"Help!" shouted Tig and hid under
the bedclothes.

"Hey Tig," I said. "Things can look scary and different at night. Some things may not be quite what they seem."

"But I can see monsters on the ceiling," said Tig.

"Why don't we look again?" I said. "Let's see what those hairy monsters could be."

"There's your new lamp, and if you look just above your new lamp you will see your fluffy sheep mobile. Round and round they go."

You made me smile!

"And if you look over there you will see . . . yes, oops, the big hairy monsters . . ."

"Round and round they go, just like the sheep. Because that's what the hairy monsters are. They are just the shadows of your fluffy sheep mobile."

"So there's nothing scary," I said.
"Just shadows."
"Hey, and you can make shadows too, Tig. You can make your very own shadow puppet show. Go for it, Tig. No more scaries. Have fun with the dark."

"Yes," said Tig. "No monsters, just shadows. I'll have fun making my very own shadow puppet show."

Lift me up . . . .

When Mummy and Daddy saw a big hairy monster with eight legs walking across Tig's bedroom ceiling they said . . .

"Aaaaaah!"

You made me smile!

"It's only my toy spider!" said Tig.

Lift me up

Tig likes the dark now.
Tig likes making shadow puppet shows.

Will you try making shadow puppets?

"I love you," says Tig.
"Night Night, Woolly."